PHERRA RISES

BOOK TWO IN THE LEGENDS OF MYTHERIOS

JAMES KEITH

JAMES KEITH
AUTHOR

Pherra Rises
Legends of Mytherios - Book Two

Editing Services Provided by There for You Editing
www.facebook.com/ThereForYouEditing

Cover Created by Rene Folsom with Phycel Designs
www.phycel.com

SYNOPSIS

Every one thousand years a beast rises from the lava-filled volcano of Mytherios. Emerging from a portal left open by The Dark Goblin, her fiery wings beat against the sky as her fury is unleashed on the world.

The perfect life Jake and his girlfriend Cassie knew is forever changed the day a strange shadow swooped overhead.

Farm animals go missing.

Property is scorched.

All by a creature once rumored to be myth.

Embarking on the adventure of a lifetime, Jake and Cassie vow to take down the creature comprised of fire and brimstone. Can they defeat the ancient beast? Or will they suffer the same fate as the thousands who challenged the monster before them?

From author James Keith comes, *Pherra Rises*, the highly anticipated sequel to his gripping novel, *The SpellMaster's Book*.

CONTENTS

SHE RISES FROM THE ASHES OF THE VOLCANO OF Mytherios every thousand years. Wings beating against the sky, her mass blocks out the sun. She's destroyed armies and conquered civilizations.

History calls her Pherra, and fabled myths whisper she is a phoenix.

Over the millennia, she claimed thousands of souls. Armies tried and failed to conquer her. Those daring enough to challenge Pherra met an untimely death. Few survived her fury. It was through them that her legend was born.

An ancient script was buried inside of the deepest, darkest mountain in Mytherios. The ancient texts that were written on the script by the Mytherios elders stated that there were four warriors who would bring hope to the world. These four would conquer Pherra and end her savage reign.

Now it was time for the four divine warriors to be freed from their prison entrapped in the mountain. They were: the Wolf Rider, the Warrior, the Mysterious Woman, and the Rhino. These warriors would stand tall together once more and defeat the evil that darkness that reigned over the once peaceful lands of Mytherios.

Pherra would rise again, the exact date unknown. If she was not stopped, millions more would die. The shadow of the phoenix was upon us.

In the land of Mytherios, a young stranger walked along the beach. A visitor to that realm, he glanced to the sky and screamed out in frustration; he was trapped and wanted to find a way back home to his family. It was his presence which woke Pherra. She took to the sky with flaming wings and burned as bright as the sun. The land of Mytherios had been silent as a tomb. Now the sound of Pherra's enormous flapping wings echoed throughout the valley below. Curious to see more of the mysterious person walking the shoreline, Pherra swooped down from above.

Suddenly, she was distracted by the vibrant colours of the void that the Dark Goblin had created, its presence drawing her in. Taking back up to the sky, she flew towards the void as it slowly drew her into another world. The strange visitor gazed up in the sky as the air rippled and sparks of energy scattered all over the lands, falling from the sky like shattered glass. Pherra continued to fly, looking around to see that she had appeared in none other than the human dimension.

Soaring high above the clouds, she discovered a small village below. The buildings were made out of materials Pherra had never seen before, and the air was much cooler, causing the fire on her wings to start to ease. There were no mountains, no volcanoes, only a forest. This world was very different from her normal mountainous regions where she could easily hide. She had to nest somewhere, but this strange world was so alien to her. Starving and needing food, her divine quest to search for a meal was her primary instinct. Soaring high, she would stare down to the ground, searching for something large enough to satisfy her enormous size. Regardless, excitement filled her … she had a whole new world to explore. Pherra was free once again.

"HEY, bright eyes, how are you today?" called Jake as

he waved to his girlfriend, Cassie, from across the street.

"Hey, there." Cassie briefly lifted her gaze from her phone and almost tripped over a dip in the curb.

It was the last day of summer break, and Jake was happy that he had one last day before school would reopen in the morning. He could continue to spend all his time with Cassie. They were lovestruck teenagers who wanted nothing more than to be in each other's company enjoying life and having amazing adventures.

As Cassie stopped walking, Jake ran across the road, almost getting himself clipped by a car.

"Want to chill out later? I got some cool new horror flicks," Jake panted as he tried to catch his breath, before apologising to the driver of the car that he had caused to slam on the brakes.

"Sure! I am just running a few errands for my mom. I'll text you later. Got to go!" Cassie said and darted off.

Jake put his hands in his pockets, feeling like he had been shrugged off by Cassie. Shoulders hunched, he headed into the café next to him. It was a blisteringly hot day, much stickier than usual and he fancied himself a drink.

"Can I have a cola please?" Jake asked, without paying attention to who was talking to him.

"Certainly. Do you want to see our menu as well?" replied the woman who Jake had blatantly not paid any attention to.

When Jake finally lifted his gaze his mouth hung open. His server had long, brown hair, beautiful hazel eyes, and a figure a supermodel would be very proud of.

"Yeah, sure." Jake didn't want to go anywhere; this waitress had his full attention. Cassie did not even cross his mind—he wanted to find out more about this girl. What was her name? How old was she? And where she was from?

After a quick trip to the counter, the enchanting waitress placed the ice cold glass on the table in front of him.

"Here is your cola," said the waitress. "Have you had a chance to check out the menu yet?"

"Yeah, I have, but what would you recommend?" Jake asked with a huge grin.

"I would recommend the big mouth burger. Seeing as you cannot close your jaw. Now please stop gaping at me like that!" scowled the waitress who forced the words through her gritted teeth.

Jake went bright red with embarrassment. "I am sorry."

"Well, I have a boyfriend and he would not be happy if he saw you looking me up and down as you are right now," she replied as she stabbed her hands on each of her hips.

Jake could not find his words. Instead, he picked up his glass of cola and started to take small sips.

"Anything else?" she asked.

"No thanks, I'm all good," croaked Jake.

The waitress walked away and started to serve another table. Jake peered around and could see others giggling. Busted and humiliated, he quickly drank his cola and left some money on the table. As he rushed out of the café, he bumped into Cassie.

"Hey again! Are you okay?" asked Cassie. "You look flustered."

Still bright red with humiliation, Jake wanted nothing more than to get out of the area before someone told Cassie what he had done. "Nah, I'm cool. Let's get out of here."

"I can't yet. I still have some things to sort out for my mom." Cassie noticed the sweat beads developing on Jake's forehead. "Jake, are you feeling okay? You don't appear well at all."

"I'm fine, honestly. Just a little over warm." He

pulled his shirt collar from his neck, wiping the sweat from his brow.

"Go home, Jake, and get yourself some rest. I will see you tonight for a horror flick. But I'll text you before." Cassie then gave Jake a short kiss on the cheek and walked down the street towards the grocery store.

Jake turned and started his journey home. There was not a cloud in the sky. Thinking about what he could watch with Cassie that night, he paused as suddenly the heat intensified, and a huge, dark shadow blocked out the sun. Jake glanced up. There was nothing there. The skies were a brilliant cobalt blue. Quick as it came on, the shadow was gone. But what had caused the massive shadow to consume the ground all around him?

2

NOT GIVING IT ANY MORE THOUGHT OR consideration, Jake headed home. He could feel the burn on the back of his neck from the intense heat, yet didn't understand how that was possible when it had suddenly become so overcast.

He made his way over to the mirror to see what was going on; the burn was increasing in intensity. His facial expression morphed into shock when he realized the extent of the burn on the back of his neck. How was this possible? Something wasn't right. Not knowing what to do, he laid down on his bed to text Cassie. After typing out what had happened, he hit send and waited for her reply.

A beat later, she responded. **I have the same problem. There was so much sunlight, then there** was nothing but shade. It only lasted for a few seconds, but the heat melted the plastic off my handbag.

Jake's brow creased with confusion. **Are you still coming over?**

Of course, Jake. I will be there around 7 p.m. I can't wait to see you. It's been such a busy day, and I'm really sorry about what happened earlier. I had to make sure that these errands were taken care of otherwise my mother would've been seriously annoyed at me.

See you at 7, babes.

His hands shook with excitement. He was so attracted to Cassie and adored spending every moment he could with her. Preparing for her visit, he started to clean his bedroom, picking up his comics off the floor and stacking them neatly on his shelf. After that, he tackled the enormous pile of laundry his mother left it in his room and asked him to sort it out a few days ago. Jake being Jake, hadn't even noticed it ... until now.

Cassie was a clean freak; she hated anything being out. Just for her, he spent the next few hours cleaning. The last time Cassie came over she lectured Jake about what a mess his room was. This was not a memory Jake wanted to repeat. Not when he had been mortified about his smelly socks lying at the bottom of his bed.

His room now spotless, Jake checked his phone for the umpteenth time, then dressed in his best jeans and T-shirt. Jake dragged himself into his bathroom, picked up his hair gel from the shelf, and slicked back his hair. Gazing at himself in the mirror, he gave himself a sly wink.

"You are so handsome, dude." Jake loved taking care of his appearance. Cassie was beautiful, popular, and everyone loved her. She was a helpful, young lady, who went out of her way to help anyone in need. Jake wanted her to be proud of him when they were seen together in public.

Burn still irritating him, he located the aftersun lotion on the bottom shelf of the bathroom cabinet. He picked it up and read the label. *To be used on mild sunburn.*

"Can't hurt," he said to himself, and squeezed a very generous amount onto his hand. As he rubbed it onto his neck, he felt the instant cool. It was bliss. Finally, the pain started to subside. Rubbing the extra between his hands, he headed downstairs to the living room. Perched on the sofa that faced the window, he eagerly awaited Cassie's arrival.

As he waited, he turned on the television. The

news was reporting about the intense heat, announcing that temperatures reached a record 150 degrees fahrenheit.

"No wonder I got burnt," he muttered to himself.

The news reporters looked very bleak, their facial expressions showing deep concern. They would both stare at each other before focusing back on the camera for their audio cues. They continued to talk about the shadow that was cast and how the heat caused the asphalt in many roads to crack. The local woodland caught fire, but luckily it was caught in time by the fire department before it could spread.

Jake was so engrossed in listening to the news, he could see Cassie walking up his drive, his mind fully focused on listening about the strange shadow. He completely forgot to go to the door. There was a quiet knock on the door. Composing himself, Jake jumped up off the sofa. He headed to the door and gazed in the mirror at himself, adjusting his hair and shirt for the final time. Taking a deep breath, he opened the front door.

A warm blush filled Jake's cheeks when he saw how beautiful Cassie looked. She wore pink lipstick, and long lashes brushed the apples of her cheeks. Her long, blonde hair hung in waves to her shoulder blades. She had made such an effort to look good for him tonight.

"C-C-Come in," he stammered and stepped back to invite her inside. He accidentally slammed the door, causing Cassie to jump.

"Jake, what is wrong with you?"

"Nothing, I was just watching the news about the shadow."

"That horrible shadow was so hot, I got a burn on my shoulders from it," muttered Cassie as she pulled her top over her shoulder to show Jake the deep red burn.

Entering the living room, Cassie sat down with Jake and watched the broadcast on the TV. There were many victims of burns that had been reported. The reporter then stated they were cutting to a commercial break and they would be back shortly.

Cassie picked up the remote control, turning off the TV. "I'm here to see you, babe, not watch the news all night," she exclaimed.

Cassie leaned into Jake, and he happily wrapped his arms around her shoulders … only for her to cringe at the pain. "Ow, that's right on my burn."

"I'm sorry, I didn't mean to hurt you," Jake apologized.

Cassie smiled in response. "Come on, let's go out

and watch a film. That's what we decided earlier," insisted Cassie.

Jake looked at his watch. It was only 8 p.m., there was plenty of time for them to go out and have a good time.

"Sure, let's go. There are a few horror films on tonight, we never did decide on which one we were going to watch."

For a moment, Jake could see Cassie looking thoughtful; she was clearly thinking. Her stare very vacant as if her mind was in a million different places. She told him earlier that she wanted to see something tense and really scary. Jake was hoping it was because she wanted him to wrap his arms around her in comfort throughout the film.

"How about that new scary movie about the legendary minotaur that lives in the labyrinth? I have heard nothing but great things about that film. It's based on a legend from a long time ago."

This was music to Jake's ears. He was hoping that Cassie would choose *The Minotaur's Rage*. Ever since he first saw the trailer a few months back, this was a film he had been eager to see.

Jake and Cassie got their things, then slowly walked out the front door, ready for a night of fun.

Comfortable in Jake's Camaro, they headed into town. Jake glanced over at Cassie who was playing on her cell phone. Wanting to impress her, he put his foot flat to the floor, sending the car jolting forward in a burst of speed.

"Jake, what the hell are you doing?" screamed Cassie, who apparently was not impressed but rather frightened.

Jake laughed, enjoying the thrill of accelerating to 100 mph on the long straights and slowing to 60 mph for the bends.

"Please be careful! Slow down now or stop the car and I'll walk home." Her nostrils flared with annoyance.

Knowing he had taken his joke too far, Jake slowed down to the speed limit. "I'm sorry, I thought you would like it if I opened her up a bit."

"I didn't. I like when you drive sensibly." As Cassie spoke, something fell from the sky. "Look out!"

Slamming on his brakes hard, Jake steered the car off the road onto the grass, coming to a halt right before a tree.

While Jake fought to steady his breath, Cassie opened her car door and stepped outside.

"Cassie, get back in the car," Jake rasped.

"Babe, come here and take a look at this!"

Jake joined Cassie on the side of the road, his eyes bulging at the sight of the cow lying on the road.

"What the ... H-Has it started raining c-cows or something?" stuttered Jake.

"I don't think so." Slowly and quietly, Cassie inched closer to the cow.

The smell was unbearable, reeking of rotted flesh.

"Jeez, that thing stinks." Jake grimaced, and his stomach began to churn.

Cassie put her hand over her face to try and block out the stench. When she reached the side of the corpse, a scream tore from her throat. Its insides had been torn out. Blood splattered across the road. Something big attacked the cow and dropped it from above.

Jake looked up into the dark night sky, but could see nothing.

"Cassie, we need to get out of here. Whatever attacked that cow could still be around."

"There is no animal alive that could drop a cow from that height." Tears streamed down Cassie's face "Is there?"

A loud rumble sounded in the distance.

"What was that?" Jake whispered.

Not taking any chances, he grabbed Cassie by the arm and dragged her to his car. Shaking in violent tremors of fear, she was unable to belt herself in. Jake buckled her seatbelt before his own, and then started the car. Slamming down the accelerator, he sped out in a spray of gravel. Whatever was lurking in the woods was not something of this world.

Jake took each turn at top speed on the way home. He couldn't get the sound of whatever it was that he heard out of his head. Cassie remained silent, his erratic driving no longer bothering her .

"It's okay, Cassie. I'm going to get us back home." Jake reached over, grabbing Cassie's hand and giving her a comforting squeeze. However, she simply stared out the front windscreen, not speaking Jake could see the horror on her face that had been before them.

Jake pulled into his driveway and darted out of his driver's door. Sprinting around the car, he wrenched open the passenger side door to help Cassie out. With one arm protectively around her and her body trembling against his, he helped her inside. Ushering her upstairs, he eased her quaking form down on his bed. "Cassie, are you okay?"

With a vacant stare, she silently rolled toward the

wall. Jake sat down next to her and checked the news on his phone. There was nothing about cows falling from the sky. Finding peace of mind in whatever way he could, Jake laid down next to Cassie and held her tight until they both drifted off to sleep.

3

Bright sunlight burning through the open curtains woke Jake at the break of dawn. He sat up and could see Cassie still fast asleep in the same position that she had drifted off in the night before. He headed over to his window, preparing to shut his curtains, but the sound of people chattering outside caught his attention. The neighbours all stood out on their lawns and driveways talking.

I wonder what is going on? Jake thought to himself.

Then he noticed there were cars that had been upturned and crushed in the road. Smoke was billowing out into the clear blue sky from the underside of the cars, one of the cars had all four wheels still spinning. Neighbours were looking on in complete shock at the crumpled and damaged cars. As he peered closer he could see a sea of devastation that spread far and wide.

What on Earth could have caused this amount of destruction? It looked like something out of a disaster movie when the twister had been and gone.

"What the heck?" he barked.

Cassie woke with a start, bolting upright. She jumped off the bed to see what was going on and joined Jake at the window. Obviously in complete shock, she placed her hand over her mouth and gasped at what she saw. "It wasn't a dream then?" she gasped.

"No, it wasn't a dream, Cassie. That cow was real, and so is this."

"What could be doing this?" Cassie appeared to become increasingly agitated again, pacing up and down the bedroom whilst breathing heavily in through her nose. Cassie was clutching onto her chest, Jake could sense that her heart was beating so fast. The frightened look he could see upon her face, he was worried about her. "I honestly don't know. But I really want to find out." Jake pulled out his cell phone again and typed in the search engine 'what can lift a cow in the air and cars'. All that came back was large equipment such as cranes and hoists. This wasn't the right answer as the cow appeared out of the atmosphere in the countryside, where there were no large cranes or equipment.

"This can't be right, Cassie! Look ..." He showed Cassie what had come back on his phone.

She started to shake her head in disbelief. "Jake, don't you get it? Whatever is doing this can't be from this world. Remember that noise in the trees last night? Nothing that walks on this planet can make a noise that loud. Whatever it is, it's massive and does not seem to care about anything in its path."

Concerned about how she was feeling, he stared at Cassie. How was this the same girl from last night? The vulnerable girl who was in shock and had completely lost her voice? Now, here she was able to talk about the previous night and have a guess that this could be some unusual creature that did not belong in this world.

"Babe, we need to see if there are any reports of any other strange creatures lately. I was told by someone at school that there's this army of goblins that lived in the sewers in a town not far from here, and that they're led by a goblin who went by the name the Dark Goblin. I always thought that this story was far-fetched and silly. Now I am starting to believe it."

"Cassie, you really don't believe those myths and legends do you? Because that is all they are, myths and legends, there is no such thing as monsters or goblins! That is just a stupid old story from a book."

Cassie rolled her eyes at Jake. He could see the eyes rolling, he knew she was far from impressed. She walked over to the desk, pulled out Jake's laptop, and turned it on.

"Wait, what are you doing?" yelled Jake as he tried to grab his laptop. It was too late; Cassie had opened his laptop. Her eyes widened when she saw the screen. Jake had been watching videos about knitting.

"Jake, really?" she laughed.

"Hey, I was just curious to see what it was all about."

"Yeah, okay, whatever you say, Jake." Cassie minimised Jake's previous screen, and then loaded up the news page about the people who had been missing in the sewers for many years, yet they had shown no signs of aging.

Jake peered over her shoulder at the news report. There were interviews from people who had been missing for fifty years, yet they looked no older than thirty. It was strange. Wanting to learn more, Jake clicked on the video, which showed a team of investigators in the sewers in the so-called Dark Goblin's lair. The amount of evidence from the missing people to the artifacts that had been found made it appear genuine. He shook his head, not wanting to believe it. He couldn't wrap his mind around these mythical creatures that people believed existed.

"Okay, well what has a goblin got to do with eating cows, dropping them from the sky, and flipping cars?" he asked Cassie curiously.

"I never said it was a goblin doing this! What I am saying is that if the tale of the goblins is real, then maybe this is another mythical being. Something big that can fly."

Jake remembered the shadow from the other day, and how it appeared out of nowhere, bringing the intense heat along with it.

"Live news report from Sapphire Farm. Ten prize cows have gone missing, and five were found scattered around the town with what appears to be bite marks. We will bring you more on this story as we get it."

Jake decided to call it quits with the TV. The news reports were a lot to take in, and he did not want to watch anymore TV that morning. Grabbing his remote control, he turned it off.

"Fifteen cows," marveled Cassie.

"Yeah … Whatever it is, it sure is hungry," replied Jake. He made his way back to his bed and sat down; he needed to get ready for school. They both had been much louder this morning than the previous night, and he was worried that this would alert his parents to Cassie's presence. He knew that if his parents found out Cassie stayed the night he would be in serious trouble. Summer break was now over and they were due back in school in just a few hours.

"We need to get to school. But my parents are downstairs having breakfast. I need you to climb out of the window and knock on the door to pretend that you are waiting for me so we can head to school together."

Cassie raised both her eyebrows and gave him a stern look. "There is no way that I am climbing out of this window. You're just going to have to accept that they know that I stayed over. You know my mother does not mind. That is because she trusts me, babe."

"It's your father I am worried about," muttered Jake as he gritted his teeth together.

"My dad is away on business, babe. It will be okay." Cassie grabbed the door handle and made her way down the stairs. Cassie's father was very strict, he never spoke to Jake and he was very concerned that if her father knew about her staying over she would not be allowed to see Jake anymore.

Jake's heart hammered in his chest. What were his parents going to think? They would never allow him to have a girl stay over in his room overnight. He quickly followed Cassie down the stairs but he couldn't stop her, it was too late. She walked straight into the kitchen.

"Good morning," she said softly.

Jake's parents glanced up from the table. Looking across the table he could see a smile on his father's face. But his mother was frowning; she was evidently unimpressed by the sight of Cassie standing in her kitchen.

"Morning, young lady," replied Jake's father.

Cassie sat down at the table, and Jake soon followed by sitting beside her. His father set the newspaper down on the table. The front page caught Jake's eye. There was a picture of a cow that had been killed, with the headline, "Who is the mysterious cow killer?" Seeing the front page took him back to the night before; he could still hear Cassie's screams of horror from when she saw what had happened to the poor animal.

"How are you this morning, Cassie? Did you stay

here overnight? Is everything okay at home?" asked Jake's father.

"Yes, I did. I stole Jake's bed and he slept on the floor. He's such a gentleman. There is no trouble at home, we got back late from the movies and I did not want to wake my mother," she answered.

Jake smiled. He was glad that Cassie did not say they had slept in the bed together, but he could still see his mother gritting her teeth. She didn't believe Cassie.

His father was always able to calm his mother and talk her down in difficult situations, and he was hoping that whilst they were at school he would do this. He really did not want to come home to a million questions from his mother.

"Don't you both have somewhere to be?" said Jake's mother very sarcastically.

"Yes, Mother. We will head to school now. We don't want to be late on our first day back." Jake stood up from the table and glanced at Cassie. He was feeling uneasy, his stomach in knots, she followed him out the back door and into the backyard.

"Nice to see you both," she shouted back to his parents.

"Why did you have to do that?" snapped Jake. He was very upset and concerned about the situation that

Cassie had put him in with his parents. His fists were clenched and he started to go ruby red in the face with anger.

"I don't believe in liars and you know that. Best to be honest and truthful," she replied.

Jake could not stay annoyed when he knew Cassie was right. If his parents had barged in and found them in his bed together he would have ended up grounded for a month.

"Best get you home so you can grab your school bag."

Cassie and Jake headed around the side of the house. The fire department had arrived to help remove the debris scattered all over the street. The noises screeching in the air from the cars was incredible. The car was flipped over by the crane and lifted on to the removal van. Finally the air went quiet, an eerie sound of silence. All the upturned cars that had been scattered along the road had finally been moved. The sweeper was out sweeping the shards of glass that lay in the road, glistening every now and again. The smell of burnt rubber and fuel was overpowering; it was making the firefighters cough unexpectedly as they smothered it so the smell lessened and the risk was gone. The smoke had masked the air, making it look as if it was a deadly night. Keen to get to Cassie home, Jake opened the passenger door for Cassie to get in. He got in the driver's seat. Looking back at the fire department tending to the mess around them, he started his engine and backed the car out of the drive. The short way to Cassie's was blocked by the fire department, and there was an array of emergency vehicles.

"Looks like we are going to have to go the long way." Jake grimaced.

"But, we will be late for school," wailed Cassie.

"Not much I can do. They have closed the road. I can't drive around this." Jake drove down the road and back towards the woods, where they had seen the cow last night. He really did not want to take this route and risk the cow still being on the road. His anxiety was raised, yet Cassie—appearing to be oblivious to where they were heading—was texting away on her phone.

The lane was clear, hardly any cars had passed in the opposite direction. Cassie was too distracted with her phone to notice where they were. Jake turned the corner slowly in hope that when he got around the bend the cow was no longer there. To his surprise, there was nothing, not even a trace that anything had been there the previous night. "How did they clean that up so fast?" he muttered.

"Huh, clean what up?" Cassie glanced up and must have realised where they were because she started to pant; she was struggling to catch her breath.

"I don't want to be here. We need to go!" she cried in urgency.

Jake hadn't sensed that they were in danger.

"Don't you hear the rumble? It's getting closer, Jake! That was the sound I heard just before we saw the dead cow."

Putting his foot down on the accelerator, Jake sped down the road. After a few minutes, he arrived at the intersection where he could turn into Cassie's estate. He pulled up outside of her house, allowing her to jump out of the car and run to the front door. As she reached for the doorknob, the door opened. Her father stood in the doorway with a very cold stare, his hands on his hips.

"Where have you been? It's obvious you were not here last night. And don't start with that 'you were away on business'. Because obviously I was at home, and *you* weren't. Where on Earth were you? With him?" He stared straight at Jake.

Jake could feel the intensity, and this sent chills down his spine. The door quickly closed, and Jake sat there in his car waiting for about ten minutes until

Cassie returned with a fresh set of clothes on and her school bag.

"Is everything okay?" he asked as she climbed into the car.

"Yeah, everything is fine." Cassie did not look at Jake; instead, she kept her head down.

He knew that there was something wrong, but he did not want to pry. Pushing his clutch to the floor and pressing his ignition switch, the car roared to a start and they headed off to school, running thirty minutes late. Jake was worried that this would result in detention, but taking the day off would not go down well if his parents found out.

4

FINDING A PARKING SPOT PROVED DIFFICULT. Jake was usually early for school and never had this issue. However, at this time of morning it was jam-packed. He drove around the lot three times with no luck.

"Just drop me off here and go and park on the road or something," insisted Cassie, as she hated being late for school.

Jake stopped the car and allowed her to get out. Following her advice, he drove out of the lot and parked on a side street. Jake loved his car and hated the fact that he had to resort to this. It was his pride and joy—a birthday present given to him by his family on his seventeenth birthday. He glanced back at his car as he walked away towards the school.

"Stay safe, princess," he said as the car disappeared out of view. He headed into school and down the empty hallway towards his history class. Jake could see through the window in the door that the lesson was in full swing. He opened the classroom door and made his way inside.

Everyone stopped what they were doing and stared at Jake.

"Good of you to join us, Mr. Henderson," said Mrs. Fieldston very sarcastically. She was an old-school teacher; she had once taught Jake's father when he was in school. Mrs. Fieldston had curly, short, grey hair and was always very firm with the class.

Jake dropped his head and looked at the floor as he walked over to his desk and sat down. Opening his textbook, he attempted to focus on the lesson. It was a struggle, as he was haunted by the images of the cow and the roaring sound that he heard in the trees.

"Pssst, Jake," Gavin called Jake from behind.

Jake turned, glancing over his shoulder. Gavin held up his phone with the news report about the missing and dead cows.

"What do you think about this? Looks like we got a serial cow killer on the loose," snarked Gavin as he started to laugh at his own joke.

This was the last thing Jake needed to see at that

moment in time. The sight of it caused stomach bile to scorch up to the back of his throat. "Not now, Gavin."

"Mr. Henderson, is there something you would like to share with the rest of the class?" asked Mrs. Fieldston, who stared down at Jake over the top of her glasses with a cold, menacing stare.

"No, ma'am," he replied.

"Well, I suggest you pay attention, since you have already missed half of the class today. If you would like, you can sit the rest of the class in the principal's office."

Jake went beet red in the face and looked around; everyone was staring at him again! Feeling the blood rushing to his cheeks as they got redder and redder, his face became hot, the droplets of sweat appearing on his brow from being humiliated in front of the entire class. Jake slumped down in his chair and folded his arms. He just stared straight on at Mrs. Fieldston for the rest of his lesson.

The bell rang, and everyone stood up and headed out of the classroom. Jake grabbed his bag and was caught by Gavin. Gavin was short and a little overweight, but always had a great sense of humour. He wanted to put a smile on everyone's face. He had a good sense of humour that masked how insecure he really was. "We should investigate this. You know I love a good mystery."

"Yeah, sure, but not right now. I have to meet up with Cassie." Jake tried to leave the classroom before he was called back by Mrs. Fieldston.

"Not so fast, Mr. Henderson. I would like a word with you."

Jake could feel the hairs on the back of his neck stand on end. He did not like the sound of this. Turning around, he made his way over to the teacher. She was sitting at her desk flicking through test papers that the class had completed before the summer break.

"Yes, ma'am" he said softly.

"I'm concerned. You arrived late today and your mind did not seem focused. This is not you, you are always giving 110% in your lessons. Is there something bothering you?" she asked, putting down the test papers on the desk and placing her hands together, giving Jake her undivided attention.

Jake let out a huge sigh of relief. For a moment, he thought he would be spending the afternoon in detention. He had never had detention before. His thumping heart had started to slow; the sick feeling in the pit of his stomach quickly faded away by what Mrs Fieldston had just asked him.

"No, ma'am, I just had a bad night's sleep. I will be my old self again soon."

"For the sake of your permanent record, I hope so," muttered Mrs Fieldston.

Jake really wanted to explain what he had seen, but he knew that she would not believe him. His story was too far-fetched. Anyone he told would think that he was going crazy.

"Come on, Jake, let's go and have some fun at the arcades," shouted Gavin as Jake left the classroom.

"What if I told you that something was eating these cows and dropping them from the sky ... would you believe me?" asked Jake, knowing no one would believe him.

"You mean like a dragon or something?"

"I guess so." Jake shrugged.

"Of course, bro." Grabbing Jake by his arm, Gavin pulled him into the science storage room. Gavin checked around and closed the door, obviously not wanting anyone to hear what he had to say. "Have you not heard of the story of the Dark Goblin? That was not really far from here. People say that the person who challenged the goblin had magical powers and that they vanished with the goblin and are still missing."

This was the same story that Jake had heard from Cassie. Was this a coincidence or did something mythical actually happen in a nearby town?

"I heard that. I did not want to believe it, but now I have it again I am starting to think that something has definitely happened."

Gavin put his arm around Jake, and he started to tell him about some of the mythical creatures he had heard about. The Dark Goblin and the mythical dragon but he didn't appear to be interested. That was until he mentioned the giant phoenix called Pherra, who every one thousand years awoke from her volcano carrying the fiery volcanic heat on her wings. He seemed to start to listen more and wanted to know everything about her, the size of her, what happened when she appeared, and if there was heat! He knew he had a book that contained more information in the back in his bag. They decided they would go and get it and see if the pieces of the jigsaw puzzle were beginning to fit together.

They retrieved the book and there it was: Pherra, a large-sized creature, appearing from nowhere, and heat from her wings.It was this last bit that made them both suddenly realise that they may have their creature.

"Heat from the wings ... that's it! That shadow that day when everyone felt the intense heat. It must have been Pherra. It is all starting to make sense now," wailed Jake.

"Slow down, Jake. These are stories and rumours. It does not mean that this Pherra is wreaking havoc with the cows in our town," laughed Gavin. "I think we need to go to city hall and see if there are any more clippings of sightings that have been documented."

"I need to find Cassie, I'll catch you later."

Running up and down the halls, he was frantically trying to find Cassie. Having to navigate the busy, long hallways was not easy. There were students everywhere. He glanced up and down. He really needed to talk to her about what Gavin had just told him.

"Jake, what are you doing?"

He stopped; the sweet voice of Cassie was right behind him.

"I have been searching for you everywhere" remarked an exhausted Jake.

Cassie giggled

"What's so funny?"

"You should have just come to my locker. I was standing there the whole time. It was so funny watching you run up and down the hallways."

Jake began to grin, then laughed. He wanted to be mad, but how could he? Her big, beautiful eyes warmed his heart. Grasping Cassie by the arm, he pulled her away from the lockers.

"Remember that story you told me about the one with the goblins?"

"Yeah, I do, and you laughed at me about it."

"Well, Gavin and I have been doing some extra research about what the mystery creature could be. We have some stuff I borrowed from the library and we plan to visit city hall. Gavin and I believe it is Pherra. I believe you." Cassie's smile turned into a frown, which concerned Jake. "What's wrong? I thought you would be happy knowing I believe you."

Cassie tutted, turned to her locker, and started to open it.

"It shouldn't take Gavin telling you something for you to believe me. You should have believed me from the start." She placed her books in her locker and then closed it. As she turned around, she tried to brush him off him and walk past him.

"I'm sorry," he said quietly.

"It's okay. I need to get my next class. I'll text you

later." Cassie flicked her hair over her left shoulder and headed down the long hallway to her class.

Still standing by Cassie's locker, Jake was in a world of his own.

"You coming, bro? Yo, Earth to Mr. Sleepy." Gavin was waving his hand in front of Jake's eyes.

"Yeah, what's up?" replied Jake after snapping out of his trance.

"We got a science class to get to."

"Oh, yeah sure." Jake and Gavin walked into the science room and sat down at their desks, ready for the next lesson to begin.

As they were waiting for Mr. Strife, the science teacher, to arrive, the whole room suddenly shook.

"Earthquake! Everyone get under your desks," shouted Gavin.

The vibration throughout the room was profound. Test tubes and apparatuses fell to the floor, shattering into thousands of pieces. Then there was the roar; it was ear-piercing. Everyone except Jake placed their hands over their ears. This was the sound he had heard the previous night.

"This is no earthquake," Jake muttered to Gavin as they were both huddled under the desk.

"I heard that, too."

They both came out from under the desk. The

tiles on the ceiling had cracked, and one of the light fittings had come loose, swinging from the ceiling with sparks of electricity hitting the floor.

Jake walked over to the window. Through it, he could see a shadow of what looked like an enormous bird with its wings spread out. He stared at the shadow, and bursting from the clouds and out of what appeared to be fire, it was there. This enormous, red phoenix in the sky. Her wings were flame red fully stretched out; it must have had a wingspan as long as two school buses. The flowing red wings were scorching the grass as it flew over. It was magnificent, yet truly terrifying at the same time.

"Pherra," he said to himself.

Gavin came running over. "Whoa, it's really real."

As quickly as they saw the phoenix it was gone again, leaving behind the scorched grass from the heat of its wings.

"Where did it go?" Jake ran over to the next window which was left wide open and poked his head outside, looking in all directions.

It's gone, but how?

"I don't know, but I have a feeling that is not the last that we will be seeing her."

Jake and Gavin then looked at the classroom. The devastation that had been caused by Pherra was immense. The stools were all over the floor, and the test tubes and beakers had shattered with her piercing noise.

Gavin and Jake gazed up and could see what appeared to be the indent of a footprint. Presumably, Pherra had landed on the roof.

"Wow, if she can do this at that distance, what else can she do?" muttered Jake to himself.

5

THE DAMAGE TO THE SCHOOL BUILDING ON THE outside was clearly noticeable. There were cracks in the foundation and there was some smoke billowing out from the top of the roof. The fire alarms had been sounded and everyone was now outside looking at the damage to the building and the strange scorch marks in the grass.

"I know how to find her," Jake whispered to Gavin as he looked up towards the roof to see if she was still there.

"How?"

"We saw the footprint on the ceiling of the science lab. First, we look along the roof line to see if we can spot her, then we find the scorch marks. The skyline was empty, next to the scorch marks. It's a trail. We can simply follow them, and it should lead us right to her. You remember the saying in the old monster movies that we used to watch? Follow the path of destruction." Jake, Cassie and Gavin began to follow the scorch marks slowly, then with increasing pace, as they didn't want to lose her.

"I agree with Jake," remarked Gavin. Now they could try and find the mysterious beast and see where she was, or at least where she was hiding.

Cassie had heard the commotion and was running to find the others. "Are you both okay? I heard the piercing sound of Pherra," shouted Cassie as she ran quickly over to the pair. She was carrying a large, brown book in her hands. She had a worried expression on her face.

The trail of scorch marks had gone; there was no sign of the marks or Pherra, so they stopped their search.

"Hey, what have you got there?" Jake questioned curiously. He pointed to the book Cassie was carrying.

"I am so glad you asked! So, I found this in the library. It's about mythical creatures that hail from an ancient land called Mytherios." Cassie then sat down on the grass and she opened the first page to show Jake and Gavin what the contents were. "See here, this is the Dark Goblin, the creature we heard about not far from here. But what gets really interesting is when you turn the page." Cassie turned over the page to show an image of the phoenix that Jake and Gavin had both seen from the window. This book matched with the one that Jake had. The jigsaw puzzle appeared to be complete.

"Pherra," whispered Jake.

"Yes, that is right. It says she lives in one of the volcanoes in Mytherios. When she is released her wings remain as hot as the lava that she was resting in. I guess that explains why everything she flies over is getting burnt."

Jake and Gavin then both sat down next to Cassie. They needed to learn as much as they could about Pherra, and especially what her weakness was.

"How do we kill it?" asked Gavin

"Kill it, why would you want to do that?" replied Cassie.

"It is very dangerous, it could kill us all."

"Hold on a minute." Cassie started to read through the pages to see if there was any information on how Pherra could be defeated. "It says here that no mortal weapons can harm her."

"So that is it? We are all just going to have to let her live amongst us like a giant wild eagle?"

"No, guys, listen. It says here the Woman of Wolf, a legendary archer from the four saviours, carries an arrow which can defeat Pherra."

Jake started to tut; it was all becoming rather amusing to him, but at the same time an adventure.

"How are we supposed to find this Woman of Wolf? Where do we look, what weapons do we need? Are there any leads in the book as to where to start our search?"

"Let me read it … It says here she is entombed in the land of Mytherios, and that a chosen one, a boy, will release the four from their tomb."

Gavin and Jake stared at Cassie who was deeply engrossed in the book that she was reading.

"Cassie, you are telling us that we have to wait for this chosen one to release these legendary heroes from their tomb. That could be hundreds if not thousands of years. Does it say who this person is, where they come from, or what skills they possess?" Jake was getting agitated by this.

"No, it doesn't."

Gavin stood up. "I've heard enough. I don't want to sit around and wait whilst Pherra turned everything I knew into ash."

"We need to find this phoenix to track her down and find out where she is nesting. Even if we only slow her down, at least it is something. I'm not going to sit by and let her destroy our town, our way of life," said Jake.

"I agree, she has already killed so many cows. What happens when her food supply runs out? Does she start eating us?" Gavin began making actions as though he was Pherra and Jake was a tasty meal.

Cassie started frantically flicking through the pages of the book, but there were no answers to what the boys were asking. Shutting the book, she placed it in her school bag. She stood up to join the two boys. "Okay, let's go and find her."

"Really baby, you will come with us?"

Cassie gave Jake a heart-melting smile.

"Yes, of course. We are all in this together. Together we will do whatever we can to slow down Pherra before she can do anyone serious harm."

The three of them then started to leave the school, which was easy because the security guard was busy with the fire department. They used the outline of the fire engine and snuck out! Hopefully, it would be a while before they noticed that they weren't there. The fire department arrived to start to find the source of the smoke. They were the only ones leaving as everyone else was far too interested to see what had happened to the school.

———

THAT AFTERNOON, Cassie and Gavin gathered at Jake's house whilst his parents were still at work. They took the opportunity to come up with a plan—how and what to do when they tracked Pherra down. The book had given them a rough idea of what type of conditions were needed to find out where she was or maybe nesting. However, they needed to find a way to keep Pherra in her nest; they could not risk her destroying everything they knew and the people that they loved getting hurt.

"Okay, here is what I am thinking. We cannot get too close, her wings are red hot and we will only end up being scorched to death. We need to find her and keep track of her. When we know where she is sleeping we can go and get the police to help us," said Jake as he was pacing up and down the living room .

"That is a good idea, but I have a few concerns," replied Cassie, who was making notes on their plan.

Gavin and Jake both looked over to Cassie.

"Tell us what's bothering you, we might be able to help?"

"Do you think the police will actually believe us for a start? I mean, the whole thing is so far-fetched, right? Even if they do come with us and we show them where we think Pherra is hiding, what are they actually going to be able to do? Remember what the book said, no mortal weapon can kill her."

"The book can be wrong, they could try and shoot her," Gavin replied as he made a drink. "Ugh, all this talk is giving me a headache."

Jake could not understand why Gavin was so keen to have Pherra killed. What was the purpose?

"Gavin, what if the bullets don't work and we make her angry? She would kill us all before we could get away. I say we go soon. We follow the scorched grass that was in the school field and see if there was anything we missed before. If the trail runs cold again at least we tried."

Both Jake and Gavin agreed. They all grabbed a pair of sunglasses and headed back to school, ready for their epic adventure in trying to locate where Pherra was nesting, when she was not flying around.

THE SCHOOL WAS NOW quiet after the principal had sent all the students and teachers home. Luckily, the security guard wasn't in the post as they sneaked past it. He must be busy patrolling the perimeter, so they would have to keep an eye out for him. The fire had been extinguished, but the damage to the outside of the building remained.

"Looks like school may not be opening for a while."

The three made their way over to where the grass had been scorched. They looked forward into the distance and saw that the trail went into the fields and as far as the eye could see.

"I am surprised that no one else has done anything or even mentioned this grass being scorched." As Jake studied the marks, he was concerned.

"I guess they were just too focused on the school," Cassie remarked as she pointed to the shell of the building.

The three of them walked on the scorched grass, the crunching sound noisy underfoot. They knew that this would be a very long trek ahead of them. The border of the school had appeared fairly quickly as they walked at a brisk pace, watching out for the guard. They climbed the turnstile that took them onto the farmer's field. A lot of the corn had been scorched, but it was a near-perfect straight line. This was easy for them to navigate. They walked on the path before them. The corn on either side of them was towering over them, blocking the sunlight from hitting them, causing the temperature to drop drastically.

"It's really cold in here," moaned Gavin.

Cassie and Jake ignored him; they just wanted to get out of the cornfield. It was very eerie; there was no sound. Even the corn didn't make a swish or a swash noise. It was unreal. The air felt stuffy, as though they were inside of an ancient cupboard filled with the mist of time. The route ahead was darkened and the colder weather was giving all of them goosebumps.

Carefully they crunched their way through the cornfield. It had to be taken slowly, as they did not want to give away their presence if Pherra was nearby. The corn beneath their feet was roasted; it had been completely incinerated by the heat of Pherra's wings. Luckily for Jake, Cassie, and Gavin it had cooled down.

"Hey, look! We are coming to the end of the field. See the trees." Jake pointed.

There was a huge sigh of relief from everyone; they were so glad to see something else other than the creepy corn that had been standing over them. They started to move faster, to get the trees as quickly as they possibly could.

The trees were green, and did not look damaged. The path appeared to end at the cornfield.

"So what do we do now?" Gavin asked at the end of the trail.

"The trail ends here, so my guess is that she gained altitude to fly over these trees. We should head into the trees and follow the line that we have already been following."

Jake nodded in agreement, and the three of them looked up at the tall, bushy trees standing in their path. They slowly stepped out of the cornfield and into the woodlands, hoping that they would eventually find where Pherra was nesting.

The sound of twigs that had fallen from the trees could be heard cracking under their feet. The background noise was non-existent, not a sound to be heard—no birds or insects. This was particularly strange for the woodlands as it was usually brimming with life.

"Well, if I wasn't creeped out by the cornfield I am very creeped out now." Gavin was scared, Jake could see the fearful expression on his face. Jake was also scared, but he did not want to show any weakness to Cassie who had wandered on ahead of the two boys.

"Hey, you two, come over here. I think I have found something." Cassie stopped, staring at something at her feet.

Jake and Gavin ran over to find out what she was shouting about.

"It's a burnt branch."

"Yeah, but why here and why is nothing else burnt?" replied Gavin.

Cassie glanced around. "Guys, look," she pointed to the opening, "through the trees is a clearing, big enough for a large animal to comfortably move around in."

Both Jake and Gavin took a step forward. Was this the location that Pherra was nesting in? The three of them carefully and very slowly headed into the gap. There was an enormous rock with hole underneath it.

"That appears to be a cave." Jake moved closer towards the entrance, and the sound of heavy breathing echoed from within it.

"I think we found her," whispered Jake. "Everyone remain quiet."

Suddenly, Gavin's cell phone started to ring. The sound was loud, and the breathing turned into an almighty roar that shook the very ground that they were stood on. They all froze on the spot, terrified. Then this enormous beak poked out from the cave. Trembling and frightened, Jake was paralysed in fear. He could do nothing but stare at this monstrous beak and the eyes that followed. Pherra made her way out of the cave where she was standing only a few hundred yards away and fully extended her wings. She appeared threatening and fierce.

"What do we do?" shouted Cassie.

Jake, still frozen and in shock, could not think of anything. Suddenly, something dropped on the floor... it was a canister. It was followed by a large volume of thick smoke. Someone was there with them. The stranger grabbed Jake by the arm and pulled him over to Cassie and Gavin.

At first they were dazed by the sudden presence of the stranger, then Gavin suddenly exclaimed, "It's him! It's the one from the book, his picture was on the tomb. It can't be, can it?"

Jake and Cassie were astounded but this was no time to be deciding if it was or it wasn't, they were in peril.

"Get into the trees, follow me now!" The person had an urgency in their voice as the echo got louder.

Now was the time to trust and ask questions later —their life depended on it. Everyone followed the stranger's voice and safely made it back into the trees. When they got out of the smoke, they turned to look behind them. The thick smoke had gotten them away from Pherra, they could hear her huge wings flapping as she took to the sky and flew away. Jake then turned back to the stranger. He wanted to know was he really the man who had been trapped in the tomb? The stranger froze and looked at the group. Each of them were eager to know who had just saved them.

6

"WHO ARE YOU? WHAT WAS THAT SMOKE YOU used?" Jake asked.

The stranger then removed their hood and face mask. To their surprise, it was a young, teenage girl—younger than Jake, Gavin, and Cassie.

"My name is Josie, and that smoke saved your lives. You don't need to know what it was." She rolled up her sleeves and brushed off the dirt that was covering her forearms.

Jake wanted to know more about this strange girl who had just appeared out of nowhere,

"Who are you, Josie? And how did you know about Pherra? Have you been following us?"

Josie walked up to Jake and looked him in the

eye. "I am a monster hunter ... I look for these mythical beasts and I hunt them down. I have not been following you. In fact, you being here messed up my chances of trying to find a way to get my brother back."

"Your brother? What happened to him?" asked Cassie.

"My brother, Andy, was on a mission to find the Dark Goblin a few months ago. We found him and his goblin army, but he got away through a portal. My brother followed him into the portal. I'm trying to find a way to reach him and bring him back. This means I need to find a portal to find my brother," she explained as she paced up and down.

"Wait, what? You were there? I have heard about this Dark Goblin, and it was in the book we saw the other day. The book had a whole chapter dedicated to the Dark Goblin. Everyone says the boy that fought him had magical powers. It was all over social media, too. Everyone was talking about it, but I just thought it was maybe someone trolling." Jake was keen to learn more. If Josie was who she said she was, then perhaps they had a chance to defeat Pherra—or at least banish her back to where she came from.

"Yes, Andy did have magical powers. It took a

battle with the Dark Goblin for him to figure it out. But he was not the only one." Josie then turned and focused her attention on a broken branch on the floor. She held out her hand and closed her eyes. Out of the tips of her fingers came some blue energy, which incinerated the branch into thousands of tiny pieces.

Everyone jumped; they could not believe what they had seen. This strange power was truly terrifying yet magnificent at the same time.

"What else can you do?" inquired Gavin, who was jumping up and down and flapping as he became more excited at what she could do.

Josie turned to Gavin. "Run towards me."

Unsure of why, Gavin ran at Josie. She extended her hand once again. Gavin stopped in his tracks, frozen still. Jake and Cassie looked from one to another in amazement, then they looked at Gavin. His eyes were not moving. It was as if time had stopped for him. Cassie started to become concerned that he may not be breathing.

"What are you doing to him? Let him go," pleaded Cassie.

Josie could see Cassie's fear and dropped her arm to her side. Gavin snapped back to his old self.

Glancing to his hands, he shook out his feet. "That was incredible! I remember the whole thing. I could still hear, see, breathe, and smell, but I couldn't move. It was like I was paralyzed or something."

Tears filled Josie's eyes, causing them to glimmer. "These powers are useless. I cannot open a portal and they will not bring Andy back. I am hoping that the phoenix will lead me to my brother. It did not arrive here by accident. So if it came through a portal, there must be another one to get it back." Josie walked away without another word, heading deeper into the woodlands.

"Wait, where are you going?" shouted Jake.

"I am going to track this phoenix."

"Can we come with you? We really want to help."

"Keep up. You fall behind and you get left behind."

The trio gathered their gear and followed Josie into the woods. The hunt for Pherra was on, and now they had a secret weapon to use. Jake felt a lot more confident with Josie around; he almost felt invincible.

―――――――――――

Josie kept very quiet with seldom a word spoken.

It seemed as if she was in deep thought as they rambled through the woods. She was exceptionally light on her feet, not causing any noise while she walked. Josie would occasionally stop and look up at the sky whenever she heard a sound. Jake was side by side with Cassie, whilst Gavin followed on from the back.

"Do you think we will find her again?" Jake whispered to Cassie.

"I'm not sure, I think we may have blown our only chance today. Pherra can cover a vast amount of ground a lot faster than we can. She may even be in another town."

Hearing Cassie and Jake talking behind her, Josie spun on them. "Pherra is here, there is a nest. She will not be far, you must stay alert at all times. It could sweep in at point in time and take one of us away in the blink of an eye."

Gavin audibly gulped. Fear apparently getting the better of him, sweat beaded on his brow.

"We need to keep moving." Josie pointed to the way ahead.

Jake looked at Gavin and shrugged his shoulders. They could not afford to lose Josie. She needed them, and they needed her. Yet Jake did not want to leave Gavin behind as they were childhood friends. "Come on, bro, you can do this. Just stick with us and everything will be okay."

"Yeah, sure …" Gavin jogged to catch up.

Josie stopped again and raised her hand in the air to indicate to everyone to halt, and they suddenly heard the flapping of wings in the distance. The faint sound of wind above them caused everyone to look up. Soaring up in the sky was a black silhouette of an enormous bird; it was bigger than a jet plane. It was Pherra, but she was too high for her to notice the four in the woodland below. Her eyes were firmly fixated on the prey she was hunting in the distance.

"She's circling her prey, but it is not us today. She is too high up. It must be something bigger than us." Josie wanted to calm the others down who had started trembling.

Cassie remembered the poor cow that she had seen on the road. She watched Pherra circle and figured it must be an animal at the farm that was on the nearside of the woodland.

"There is a farm not far from here, she will be searching for her next meal. We have to stop her, we cannot let her eat all of the livestock in town. We are going to run out of milk and food stocks for ourselves, if she continues to eat everything in sight.

The farmers have had a bad enough time with the recent hurricanes destroying last year's crops."

Josie nodded at Cassie; she agreed.

"Lead the way then, which path do we take?"

Cassie led the way through the woods towards the farm. She stopped and looked at Jake, indicating for him to come and join her at the front. Taking the hint, Jake ran forward and caught up with Cassie.

Jake could hear Cassie's heart hammering against her ribs, and could see the hairs on the back of her neck standing up as he stood close to her. He took her by the hand and was shocked at how cold her hands were; they were clammy and her fingers were trembling.

"Hey, it's going to be okay. We have real backup now," said Jake softly, and dotted a kiss to the back of her hand.

"I know, but I never expected Pherra to be so massive," Cassie croaked.

They continued to walk for about ten minutes. In the distance they could see the large barn that was situated on the farm.

"We are almost there," called Cassie.

They both stopped, and Josie joined them at their side. They looked around and saw a very red Gavin, who was severely out of breath trying to catch up.

"Come on, we have no time to waste," Josie insisted.

"Seriously, I am exhausted," moaned Gavin, trying his hardest to keep up with the group.

As they exited the woods, a large shadow cast over the far side of the barn. The horses ran around their paddock, terrified by what was above them. Josie sprinted ahead. Pherra was much lower now, and the growing summer heat and the burning of a thousand suns could be felt from her wings.

"Damn, that's gonna burn you alive if it gets you!" shouted Jake as he pulled Cassie back from getting burnt. They took cover to try and shield themselves from what felt like the fires of hell. It was hard as the heat was so intense, like nothing they had experienced before. The animals were all making loud noises, scared by the creature above and the scorching temperature. Unfortunately, they were trapped within their enclosures, and only those in the field could escape into the woodlands. True fear was expressed on their faces. Gavin was running across the field, having fallen behind once again.

"Gavin, come on. Hurry up!" shouted Jake.

Pherra appeared, her ravenous gaze fixed on Gavin.

"Gavin, move! She's right behind you," Cassie screamed her throat raw.

Josie turned around, raised her hand, and fired a blast of blue energy directly at Pherra.

The blue energy hit Pherra, yet still she kept on swooping down. No one understood why the blue energy hadn't worked. Pherra, with her huge wings spread wide, claws ready to grab Gavin, continued on her path for him.

"Do something!" screeched Cassie at the top of her voice.

The group came together to stand around Gavin to protect him.

Josie then, with all her power, pointed towards Pherra and froze her in mid-air.

"Hurry! I cannot hold her! She is too strong," screamed Josie, her knees buckling.

Gavin sprinted for all he was worth with the others. They made it to the barn in the same instant Josie collapsed under the strain. Pherra swooped low, but there was nothing to grab. She soared back up in the air again. A weakened Josie couldn't stop her. Pherra circled the horse paddock and dove once more. This time she snatched one of the horses and carried it off into the air with her.

"Noooooo!" wailed Cassie.

The horse's cries could be heard echoing from a distance. Soon, there was silence. Jake ran over to Josie to help her up, only to discover her nose was bleeding.

"Are you okay?" he asked frantically.

Josie brushed herself off and got her feet under her. She was dazed and very confused. "I-I am n-not strong enough to kill her." Josie pulled her hood up over her head and walked away. It was obvious she was distraught with how the events turned out, and she started to kick the ground. Josie had tried everything in her power to prevail, but it was just not enough.

"What? You managed to freeze her enough to allow Gavin to get away. You are strong enough," shouted Jake as he gave chase.

Josie stopped. She turned to the others who were all grateful for what she had done. "I failed! That poor horse is probably dead because I am too weak. I need to harness these skills so that I can save the livestock, and once I've mastered the skill then we are ready to save my brother."

"I'm alive because of you. If it wasn't for you, it

could have been me and not one of the horses." Gavin ran over to Josie and gave her a massive hug—she had just saved his life after all.

Josie dropped her hood and looked at the trio "Okay, from here on out we stick together."

Side by side, they watched Pherra disappear into the horizon.

7

THE GROWL OF A LOW RUMBLING ENGINE COULD faintly be heard in the distance. The sun had begun to set and the group knew that once night fell the search would need to be called off.

"You hear that? It sounds like a truck," whispered Jake.

"I do," Cassie replied as she looked into the direction of the noise.

The group stopped, glanced at each other. They needed to get home as soon as possible.

"Josie, where do you stay? Where's home for you?" Jake questioned as they steadily walked towards the noise.

"I live with my parents, about forty minutes away from here."

"That town with the Dark Goblin was really that close?" replied Jake.

Josie nodded.

They all picked up the pace, hoping to get a ride back into town. Josie did not want to miss the last bus, and time was not on her side. The hum of the engine was closer now, accompanied by wheels crunching over grass.

"I think it's coming this way," Jake called out.

Over the hill, there were headlights. It was indeed a pick-up truck and it was headed their way. Everyone was overjoyed with the sight of the truck. They were all smiling in relief. They could get a ride back into town and no one would get into trouble for being out so late. As the truck neared, the ground began to shake. The vibration threw the group off guard, and they began to lose their balance; their walk turned into a trip and tumble. The sky exploded with a flash. Flaming red wings beat against the air. Pherra dipped into a dive and extended her talons, piercing through the roof of the truck. Shrieks rose up as Pherra lifted the truck off the ground. Soaring skyward, she ascended with the truck in tow. The weight of the truck tore the roof off in a screech of metal and the vehicle plummeted to the earth. It hit the ground with a mighty crash, throwing bits of debris across the field.

"Oh my God, we need to help them!" Cassie burst into tears; she had never seen anyone killed before.

Their group ran very quickly to the truck, finding it compacted from impact. Glancing around, they found no sign of anyone.

"Can you kids tell me what that was that destroyed my truck?" a shaky voice ventured.

There, on the floorboards of the truck, hunkered Herman the farmer.

"Oh thank goodness you're okay!" Cassie blubbered.

"That was Pherra, she's a phoenix, a very dangerous one at that." Jake put his hand out to retrieve Herman's hat.

"A phoenix here? I guess that explains a lot!"

Jake and Gavin both helped Herman back to his feet. He picked up his shotgun that he had managed to grab before hunkering on the floorboard.

"How did you manage to get out?" asked Jake tentatively.

"Well, when the windows shattered, the truck started to lift, so I grabbed my gun and hauled myself out of there. I may be an old farmer, but I am not stupid. Then you came to my aid. Now, where is this phoenix you are telling me about? I got a score to settle." Herman loaded his shotgun and got it ready to fire.

It was very quiet, not a sound in the air.

As if cued by his question, a mighty roar sliced through the night. It made the very ground shake beneath their feet. Pherra landed right behind them, her wings stretched out wide to show off her massive size. All they could do was gape in disbelief.

Herman was the first to snap out of his shocked stupor. Aiming his shotgun, he fired directly at Pherra's head. Pherra shook it off and stared straight through Herman, as he reloaded his shotgun.

"Josie, do something." Jake tugged at her arm to get her to react.

Josie raised both her hands and tried to move her arms to fire at Pherra but she couldn't. "We need to run, I cannot do anything," she wailed. "I'm still weakened from earlier. My magic is no use."

Herman managed to reload his shotgun and took another shot, this time aiming at Pherra's wing. Pherra folded in her wings to deflect the shot; it bounced off and into the distance. She then stared at Herman, opened her enormous beak, and let out another huge roar which sent everyone crashing to the ground. As Herman started to reload, he sat up. Pherra was moving closer and closer, so close that now she was towering over him. She picked him up in her strong, majestic beak and threw him into the air, before flying up and catching him in her tight grip.

"Help me," shouted Herman as Pherra flew off into the distance. His pleas for help soon turned into blood-curdling screams that faded away.

Cassie froze to the spot and started to shiver uncontrollably, then tears began to flow. "How many more losses will there be?"

Jake put his arm around her, but she pushed him away. He was lost in his own thoughts. He was angry now. Before he had been annoyed, now he was beyond vexed as he clenched his fist tightly.

As for Gavin, for once the wise guy couldn't come up with a wisecrack. He simply said, "We've come too far to be defeated, let's move on ... there was nothing anyone could do to help Herman."

All that remained was his shotgun, which he had dropped, and his hat that had fallen off when he was flung into the air. Gavin picked up his gun. "This could be handy."

It seemed as if Cassie was coming back to her senses and calm had come over her.

Josie spoke to Cassie, "We need to get out of here. This is too dangerous, we are all going to get killed. We need to come up with a better plan, so we are prepared and we have the equipment we need. Now we have more knowledge and we can be armed better. It's time to go home, rest, regroup, and reassess, and then deal with it!"

Jake came over to reassure Cassie and to back up what Josie had said. Once they were all rested, had planned, and had the right equipment, then they could find Pherra.

Josie said, "I know that we're outmatched. Like the Dark Goblin, Pherra's practically immortal and my magic's no match for it, but I also know there's an answer as to how we can and will get her."

———————

THEY ALL DECIDED to walk back to town, Herman's death weighing heavy on their troubled minds. It took a few hours for them to reach the outskirts of town. There was no way around it now, they would be in trouble for staying out after their curfews. *But in the grand scheme of things, does it really matter?* thought Jake.

"See you all tomorrow?" he asked.

"Yeah, unless I'm grounded. I better get home fast," replied Gavin

"Okay, babe." Cassie rose on her tiptoes and gave Jake a kiss.

"What about you? Where are you staying tonight, Josie?" asked Jake.

Josie looked at her watch and realised that she missed her last bus. "Looks like I am on the streets tonight. My parents are going to be worried sick."

Jake twiddled his thumbs nervously. He could not leave Josie out on the streets all night, but his parents wouldn't be thrilled. Still, he had to help.

"Josie, why don't you text your parents and tell them you are staying at a friend's house tonight? You could come and stay with me."

Jake's comment earned an icy cold stare from Cassie.

"Jake, can I please have a word?" Cassie grabbed his sleeve and yanked him aside.

"Listen, Cassie, I know you aren't happy about the situation, but we cannot leave her out in the cold all night. It's freezing cold out here." He pointed to damp dew that was beginning to appear.

"I know that, Jake, which is why she should not be staying with you. What if her parents call and want to check? What are you going to do? Are you going to pretend to be a girl?"

Jake let out a sigh. Cassie was right. "Well, what do you suggest that we do then?"

"She stays with me. My parents won't mind, and they will just think that we are having a girly sleepover."

"Great idea, Cassie! I love you so much." Jake gave Cassie a kiss on the cheek. "Josie, go with Cassie. She will take good care of you tonight."

Josie nodded and followed Cassie down the street. Jake then headed home, hoping not to get in a world of trouble when he walked through the front door. He checked his phone as he walked; he didn't have any missed calls or texts from his parents. He felt confident everything was going to be okay … until he realised he left his car on the side street outside of the school.

"Oh man," he muttered under his breath as he unlocked the front door and tiptoed inside.

His parents were sitting in the lounge watching TV with their backs to him. Jake carefully closed the door and crept up the stairs to his room. Once in his room, he quickly got changed into his pajamas and climbed into bed. Jake's parents were downstairs talking; they had not noticed that he was back late. He felt so relieved.

He sent a message off Cassie to ask how she was getting on with Josie.

She responded, **All is well.**

Next he received a photo. It was Cassie and Josie both sitting on her floor, reading the large, brown book that Cassie found earlier in the day. Wanting to know all he could about Pherra, he asked Cassie to take pictures of a couple of the pages and send them to him. He noticed there was a reference to *The Spellmaster's Book*.

One by one the pictures came through, and he lay there on his bed reading through the texts. His mood sank lower and lower when he realised that there was very little they could do to cause Pherra any harm. Time and again the book stated only the Wolf Rider could truly defeat Pherra. Continuing to read, he realised they needed *The Spellmaster's Book*. This was the key; it was a book so powerful that it could cast the most complex spells. It could create portals, which was exactly what Josie and his team had been looking for. He quickly called Cassie.

"If we can find this book, perhaps we can defeat Pherra. What do you think?" He could hear the echoes from his phone. He knew he was on loudspeaker.

There was a quiet pause before Josie spoke. "*The Spellmaster's Book* is in possession of the Dark Goblin, he took it through the portal with him. That's why my brother went in after him. We have to find another way."

Feeling hope was lost, Jake simply hung up on the call.

8

As the sun poured through Jake's window he slowly opened his eyes. Bright light reflected off his bedroom mirror. Gaining focus, he picked up his phone to see if Cassie had been in touch. There were no messages. He placed his phone back on the bedside cabinet and rolled over, exhausted. He longed to have a lie in. Unfortunately, the second he closed his eyes his phone rang. Rolling back over, he picked it up. It was Cassie.

"Hello"

"Jake, you are not going to believe this but the news is talking about the destroyed truck and the missing horse from the farm. It even says that Herman vanished." Cassie sounded distressed, as if the events of the previous night were still unfolding at that current time.

Jake sat up, his eyes bulging. "Really? So does everyone know about Pherra now?"

"No, not yet. No one has mentioned anything."

Jake climbed out of bed. "What time do you want to go today?"

"Give us about an hour, and we will meet you by the old woodshed on the lane near the entrance to the woods." Cassie's breathing began to get deeper as if she were anxious about what could happen.

"Yes, of course. I will see you soon." Jake tossed his phone down on his bed, grabbed his clothes, and walked down the hall. He could hear his parents downstairs talking about Herman and how they were concerned that he was missing. Jake headed into the bathroom and got himself showered.

Once he was ready, Jake went into the kitchen where his parents were sitting at the table. The newspaper was placed on the table, the headlines all about Herman's disappearance. His father was taking sips of his coffee whilst his mother was tucking into her french toast.

"Good morning." Jake made his way over to the fridge to grab himself some orange juice.

"Where were you last night?"

Jake froze. He turned around to see his mother staring at him. "I was—"

"We know you were out late. You were with that girl, weren't you?" scowled his mother as she fixed her eyes upon his.

Jake's pulse pounded.

"Leave the boy alone, Cassie is a lovely girl. I really do not know what your problem is with her." Jake's father adored Cassie and her mild-mannered personality.

Thankful his father stood up for him, Jake sighed his relief and took his orange juice to the table. His eyes kept wandering to the newspaper, the image of the mangled truck demanding his attention. He could still hear Herman's screams as they faded away.

"I have to go," he said to his parents and bolted out the backdoor. In the driveway Jake checked the time. He had twenty minutes to get to the meeting point to see Cassie and Josie. Dialling his phone, he called Gavin. "Gavin, meet us by the old woodshed on the lane at the entrance to the woods in twenty minutes."

"Yeah, I know, Cassie called me already."

"Is she there with you now?" Jake looked around.

"Nah, just me here. No one else about. I haven't even seen anyone walking their dog yet."

"Stay where you are, I'll get there as fast as I can." Jake shoved his phone in the side of the backpack and picked up his pace, running as fast as he could. He did not want his friends to be left alone with the potential for harm to come their way.

As Jake got onto the lane, he ran hard; sweat was pouring down his forehead. Cassie and Josie were in the distance walking towards the old wooden shed.

"Hey!" he shouted.

They both stopped and turned around to see Jake charging at them at full speed. As he caught up, he leaned forward, placing his hands on his knees. He was out of breath and he was exhausted.

"Did you run like that all the way here?" asked Cassie.

"Yeah, just give me a sec," he gasped.

"Great, now we are going to have a stinker for the rest of the day," laughed Josie.

Jake rose to his feet and gave Josie a sarcastic smirk. "We need to catch up to Gavin, he has been waiting there all by himself."

"I'm sure he will be fine. It's well covered there. That's why I suggested the woodshed to begin with." The old woodshed was covered in vines and had great tree cover. The trees just off the lane were densely packed. There was no way that Pherra, as large as she was, could maneuver through the area.

The old woodshed was exhausted. As they arrived, it looked like it had not been tended to since they had last seen it the previous summer. There was much more overgrowth and it was beginning to blend in with the environment.

"A few more years and this woodshed will not be visible anymore," Gavin pointed out as everyone arrived.

"This is the perfect hideout." Josie inspected the old woodshed as she walked around its exterior. "Where's the entrance?"

"I'll show you." Jake led Josie around the side to the wooden door that appeared to be wedged closed.

"Have any of you ever been inside?" asked Josie.

Everyone looked at one another and shook their heads.

"No, none of us have ever been able to open the door. It is completely jammed shut." Jake repeatedly pulled on it.

Josie grinned, her white teeth gleaming, and told the others to move out of the way. Once they had, she stood a few feet away from the door and hit the hinge with a huge blast of blue energy. It broke loose and the door flew open. "Shall we take a look inside?"

"After you," remarked Jake. He stood out of the way and allowed Josie to walk into the woodshed.

It was almost pitch black inside. The smell of dampness hit them straight away; there was dust and spiderwebs all over the shed. The floor was solid, no one had been inside for an extremely long time. In the corner of the room, under a mountain of dust, was a large, brown blanket.

"Hey, guys, over here. I think I found something," called out Josie.

All four of them gathered around the blanket.

"What exactly are we looking at?" asked Gavin.

Grabbing the blanket, Jake tugged on it. "Hey, give me a hand. I think there is something underneath this."

Cassie, Josie, and Gavin helped Jake pull the blanket with a mighty tug. It broke free in a flurry of dust. Everyone started to cough from the dust, which was going everywhere. Then everyone went quiet when they saw the old, antique, brown box, and wondered what it held inside.

"Who is going to do the honours?" ventured Gavin.

Jake stepped towards the box, but Josie put her hand on his arm. "I'll do it. We don't know what is in that box. If it's dangerous, I could destroy it before it destroys us."

Jake agreed, and they watched as Josie knelt down on the floor. She lifted the hinge on the box and opened the lid. Inside was a golden gauntlet. It looked ancient—perhaps many thousands of years old —yet it had been perfectly preserved in the box. Josie reached in and picked it up to study its beautiful golden exterior. There were gems and jewels all over it.

"What is that?" Jake pointed to the gauntlet.

"Honestly, I don't know." Josie opened up the gauntlet and placed it on her wrist. It quickly locked itself in place and the gems lit up. Josie screamed in pain as she was lifted off the ground with bright blue light emitting from her body.

"What is going on? Jake, help her please," wailed Cassie.

Obviously having seen enough, Gavin ran outside.

Jake ran over to Josie and tried to drag her back down, but he couldn't. Plus, she was ice cold. "She is freezing, I don't know what to do."

Beams of light fired out of Josie's chest in multiple directions. Josie slowly lowered back to the floor. She looked at her arm, and tried to remove the gauntlet to no avail.

"The gauntlet is not your enemy, but your greatest ally." Josie heard a strange voice in her head.

"Who said that?" she called out.

"Who said what?" pressed Jake. "Are you okay?"

Ignoring the presence of Jake and Cassie, Josie looked around the shed to see if there was anyone there.

"The gauntlet will make you more powerful than ever before. It will magnify your powers," the voice stated in her head once again, and then faded away.

Josie raised her arm and began to fixate on the gauntlet. "Cassie, grab the book. Maybe this thing is in there somewhere."

Cassie dropped her backpack on the floor and pulled out the old book. She handed it to Josie, who skipped through the pages.

Jake saw something that caught his attention. "There! Go back a few pages." As Josie turned back the pages, there it was, a picture of the gauntlet.

"I can't believe it! How does something from an ancient land end up in this old woodshed buried under a blanket?" He glanced at the old box and the dusty blanket.

"Well, what does it say?" Cassie questioned.

"Says here ... the Gauntlet of Strength is a gauntlet used by an ancient warrior known as the hunter. The gauntlet itself magnifies your strengths and powers immensely."

Josie gasped as Jake continued to read about how it harnessed powers.

"This is good news! You may now be strong enough to take down Pherra." After Jake had spoken, Gavin popped his head around the door.

"Is it safe now?" he asked.

Everyone laughed; they had all completely forgotten that Gavin ran out.

"Yes, bro, everything is okay. So, guys, are we ready to head back to the cave?" Jake asked. "We have a monster to slay."

Josie nodded and was first to leave the woodshed. The remaining three stepped outside. Behind them, from the direction of town, came an almighty roar. Slowly, they turned.

"Looks like we don't have to find her after all." Jake looked up to the sky.

In the distance, they could see Pherra circling over their town. She had brought the fight to them.

9

FEELING STRONG AND CONFIDENT, THEY WALKED down the lane and back to town. This time Pherra was not going to get away so easily. Josie told them that she could feel deep inside of her that she was stronger now. She wanted her brother back and was going to stop at nothing to find a way to make that happen.

As they got closer to the town, they could hear the panic that Pherra was causing. Car horns beeped. People were screaming.

"Now everyone knows she is real," Jake remarked as he listened to the horns and the people screaming in the distance.

The sound of wailing sirens closed in. The group

pushed on as fast as they could to try and help their family and friends. They had lost Herman, losing anyone else was not an option.

The town was full of people running around with their gazes locked on the sky. Their cries were deafening as they dove for shelter inside of any building they could. There was pandemonium everywhere. The roads had been gridlocked with people trying to get out of the town. Up above, Pherra circled in search of her next meal.

"Guys, we need to distract her, get her away from the town—" Jake's idea was cut short by sirens tearing down the sidewalk.

Four police cars screeched to a halt, officers scrambling out of each. One look at Pherra and they pulled their weapons.

"Wait, no!" shouted Cassie, but it was too late.

The police opened fire at Pherra, their bullets not doing anything to stop the phoenix from swooping across the sky.

"Fire at its wings," demanded the commanding officer.

The police focused their fire on her fiery appendages. Pherra shrieked as she landed on top of the church opposite the police cars. Jaw swinging wide, she let out a deafening roar that shattered the windows of all the surrounding buildings. Thousands of shards of glass rained down on the officers and civilians below.

Once more Pherra soared to the heavens

"Everyone okay?" shouted the commanding police officer.

The other police officers nodded, indicating that they were fine.

The commanding officer picked up his radio. "We are going to need military support here, as there is an extremely large bird and our weapons are proving ineffective. Send air support and whatever you have available, we need support now!"

Josie shook her head at the officer's requests. This was not going to work. She looked at the gauntlet. "Let's see what this thing can do."

As Pherra circled again in the sky, Josie raised her arm. She could feel the power of the gauntlet pulsing through her body; she felt a sense of newfound energy, flowing throughout her entire body. Josie could see the gauntlet glowing as its power struck Pherra, then froze her in mid air. Everyone stopped and stared in amazement.

The police took this opportunity to fire everything they had at Pherra, but the heavy sound of explosive gunfire was far too distracting for Josie. Concentration slipping, she lost her hold on Pherra. The phoenix flew off. Swooping down, she lifted one of the police cars with her claws before throwing it into the office block behind them, causing it to explode.

The heat from the explosion was like a furnace that had been working over time. It was so hot the road was beginning to melt; you could smell the tar in the air. The sound of the explosion was horrific, and had left Jake with a ringing in his ear. Jake pulled Cassie to the side of the road and on to the grass to shield her from flying debris from the blast.

Gavin watched on in shock, not able to move, as a small part of metal came off a car flying through the air at great speed. It hit Gavin like a bullet, puncturing his leg. Screaming in immense pain, he immediately crumbled and fell to the floor as the blood started to gush. Pherra stopped in the air; she could smell the fresh blood ...

Turning her head, she looked straight down at Gavin on the earth. Her bright red wings flapped to gain speed, then she dove down like a peregrine falcon. Josie jumped in front of Gavin and tried to freeze Pherra with the gauntlet but she couldn't; she was still weakened from using her powers before.

Pherra scooped up Gavin off the ground who began screaming at her to let him go.

Josie grabbed his hand. "I have you, don't let go."

"Help me," Gavin wailed as his fingers slipped from her grasp.

Pherra continued to rise above the town and flew away.

Gavin's cries faded into the distance.

Josie fell to her knees and burst into tears in frustration. She had failed. Grabbing at her wrist, she tried to take off the gauntlet. It wouldn't move, she could not remove it. Then, before her eyes, the lock mechanism disappeared, it became solid, and it was now a part of her!

"You did all you could," sobbed Jake, who was heartbroken at the sight of his friend being carried away by Pherra.

Cassie wrapped her arms around him and held him tight. He had saved her, but no one could save Gavin.

THE SOUND of humming could be heard in the distance, then there was a huge pop. An aircraft was overhead; it was so loud that it caused the very ground to shake.

"Looks like they got their military support," Jake muttered as he pointed to the aircraft above.

Three helicopter gunships flew overhead. The three watched in the skies as they pursued Pherra.

"We need to get to the cave, stop the aircraft, and then Pherra. Gavin might still be alive." Josie was extremely insistent that they all head back to the woods. "Let's go! If we move now, we can be there before late."

"I have a much faster way." Jake, who was pacing from one foot to the other, stopped and he tried to lead the way. "Let's head to the school."

"Why?" asked Cassie, as she started to walk in a different direction. "That is way out of our way."

Jake pulled out his key fob to his Camaro. Cassie smiled. The three ran towards the school. Jake headed down the side street to his Camaro..

"Get in, guys! You need to hurry up." He buckled his seatbelt.

Josie looked at the two-seater car. "There is no room."

Cassie reached out her hand. "It will be okay, we can share a seat."

Jake fired up his engine and let it roar.

"You know, babe, I'm not going to moan about your driving tonight. Floor it, let's get there as fast as we can."

Now he had Cassie's permission and nothing was going to stop him.

"You got it." Jake slammed his foot to the floor, causing the car to wheelspin into a thick cloud of smoke before flying off down the road.

Sharing the passenger seat, Cassie and Josie clung to each other. The side streets were deserted, the majority of residents trying to get out of town on the main roads. As Jake pulled up to the junction that connected the road to the woods he saw tail lights as far as the eye could see. The traffic was jammed; so many people driving the wrong way. They were headed in the direction of Pherra.

"What the hell? Are they stupid or something? You can't just out run her ..."

"Do you know another way?" asked Cassie.

Jake bit his bottom lip, thinking. He looked in his side mirror and an epiphany hit him. "Yeah, I do. Hold on." Jake kissed her hand. Then he spun the car around and headed up the side street. At the end of the street there was an old, wooden fence that led to one of the farmer's fields.

"Jake, you're not going to do what I think you are going to do, are you?" Cassie looked terrified.

"Hold on!" Jake continued to accelerate and crashed straight through the wooden fence and into the field. He drove along the field as fast as he could. The bumps caused the car to go up and down.

Cassie looked like she was going to vomit.

Overhead, the helicopters and fighter jets could be seen flying towards the woodland. The fighter jet kept circling, waiting for Pherra to make an appearance.

"This is going to turn into a war zone any second now," muttered Jake. He continued to drive across the field, before crashing through another wooden fence and onto the lane where they had met earlier in the day. He floored it and slammed on his brakes hard and came to a stop. Cassie was just staring into space, her hair a mess and her eyes rolling over. Josie got out of the car first and vomited as she did. The sadness and anger was all coming out. Jake missed the vomit as he got out, and it just dawned on him that he had terrified Cassie.

"I am so sorry, babe."

Cassie looked at Jake and shook her head. "I take it back, don't ever drive like an idiot again."

The sound of the military aircraft overhead was

deafening. They were flying so low that it was causing disruption to the trees.

"Are we going to do this?" asked Jake to Cassie and Josie.

They both nodded as they all stepped into the woods in hope that they could find Gavin still alive.

THE SOUND OVERHEAD MADE IT EASY FOR THE three to navigate through the woods much more quickly. They followed their tracks from the previous day, led by their old footprints in the muddy ground. The overgrowth was thick, and the wind created by the helicopters above was making everything wave.

"How much farther do you think this is going to be?" asked Cassie as she looked at the road ahead.

"If I remember right, about an hour, and it's about 3 kilometres that way," responded Jake.

Josie stopped and looked at them both and shrugged her shoulders. "I wouldn't ask me, I never entered the woods this way. I came in from the other side and met you all just before you were about to become dinner."

"I don't really want to think about becoming dinner. I'm worried about Gavin. I do hope that he is okay." Cassie seemed deeply concerned.

"She's right, we need to move quickly. I just know he is still alive. I can feel it inside of me." Jake motioned to the others to keep moving.

Picking up the pace, they broke into a jog. The sound of the branches and stodgy mud under their feet was easily being drowned out by the helicopters above, which were now coming into view. Then helicopters were slowing down.

Josie and Cassie glanced up. The helicopters were hovering in place.

"I think they have located her," remarked Josie.

"Yes, I agree. We need to get moving before this place turns into a war zone," said Jake, thinking out loud.

They began to run; they knew they had to get past where the helicopters were hovering and away from them as fast as they could. As they were running, there was a huge, almighty bang, followed by a flash of bright light and a second immense explosion, which knocked all three off their feet and sent them spiralling into the sky before landing very sharpishly on the earth below. Picking themselves up off the floor, they began to run again.

"They are firing at her." Josie pointed at Pherra. A huge fireball could be seen in the distance above the trees. The fire quickly started to catch on to the trees around the woodland.

"We need to get out of here," shouted Jake.

"But we can't leave Gavin, we need to help him." cried Cassie as she tried to run towards the fire.

Jake grabbed her by both arms and held her back.

Josie stared at the destruction that was in front of them. "He's right, there is nothing we can do there now. If we continue we will all die."

A distraught Cassie started trying to move her arms and legs as she tried to pull away from Jake. He gripped her tighter, dragging her close to him, making sure he had a very firm grasp on her.

Then there was a huge roar as Pherra ascended through the fire. The missile had set alight the woodlands and it was spreading quickly. Its intended target was unhurt although Pherra was now vexed. The three helicopters fired in unison. Another three missiles came shooting out, this time hitting Pherra directly, sending her flying backwards and down into the trees.

"We need to go now," shouted Jake. The fire was sweeping through the woodlands at an alarming rate. They were in imminent danger. Jake took a step backwards, and Cassie managed to break free of his grip. She sprinted straight towards the fire, and Jake ran after her. Josie raised her arm, ready to freeze Cassie, but stopped and lowered it. She did not want to weaken herself in case she needed to use her powers at any other point. Instead, she gave chase to Cassie.

Cassie ran into the burning woodland, smoke filled the air. Jake took off his hoodie and wrapped it around his mouth and nose, trying to reduce the amount of smoke that he would be breathing in.

"Cassie!" shouted Jake at the top of his voice.

At this point, Josie had caught up to Jake. "This way, follow me!"

Jake followed her through the trees and the thick smoke. They were now at the clearing; it seemed that this was the only part of the woods that was not on fire. The cave was up ahead, and there was no sign of Pherra.

Did the three missiles actually take her out? Jake thought to himself.He looked up to see Pherra flying directly at the helicopters and realised no they didn't. They opened up their machine gun fire, but the bullets were just bouncing off Pherra. She rose to the heavens above and swooped down. The helicopters tried to maneuver but it was too late. Pherra landed on one, grabbed it, and threw it; it was circling uncontrollably. The aircraft was spinning so fast it looked as if it was still. It soon hit the ground and erupted into flames. The two remaining helicopters tried to leave, but they were not fast enough to escape Pherra.

The phoenix let out a roar that created a shockwave in the air; the trees were swaying and moving. The vibration was so powerful that the turbulence caused both helicopters to descend rapidly and crash into the ground. These two, however, did not meet the same fate as the other—there was no explosion. Pherra raised her wings in triumphant victory, then from behind there was the largest explosion of all. The fighter jet swooped in out of nowhere and hit Pherra with a missile that caused the whole sky to light up in flame red. A huge cry could be heard from Pherra who hit the ground with an almighty thump.

"This is our opportunity! She is down, let's get to the cave." Jake followed Josie to the cave. There was Cassie standing in the entrance. When they caught up and looked inside, they could see it was very dark.

"Cassie, what are you doing? You could have gotten yourself killed," asked Jake.

Cassie stared into the cave and started to walk slowly into it. "I hoped that you would come for me.

We do not leave friends behind, Jake." She gestured to him.

Jake felt extremely sombre. He hadn't thought they'd get here with everything that had been happening. He followed Cassie into the cave.

Josie held her hand in front of her, and it lit up in a stunning bright blue. "Now we have light."

Astonished, Jake and Cassie allowed Josie to take the lead. The cave was vast in its girth. It looked as if Pherra had dug it out; there were large indents on the inside that appeared to be claw marks. It was dusty, musky; the stones and soil around the walls were scorched. Most likely from the heat omitted from Pherra's wings.

The cave was expansive and its depths were coming into view, but it was perfectly straight. There were no small caverns or turns. They continued to walk slowly but with caution.

"Hey, do you guys hear that?" Jake was saying when both Josie and Cassie stopped. They remained silent, listening to see what Jake had heard.

"Yeah, it sounds like voices." Cassie then ran on ahead, eager to see if the voice she could hear was Gavin's.

As they ran they could see a small, dim light. It was a campfire with the embers glowing in the vast darkness, and sitting around the fire was Herman, Gavin, and a woman they had never met before.

"Gavin, you're okay!" shouted an overjoyed Cassie, who wrapped her arms around him, squeezing him very tight.

"Yes, I am fine." Gavin tried to wriggle free from her tight hold.

Herman then stood up and looked at the three of them, smiling as he did. "I guess that you are all here to try and save us. I wouldn't bother. We have all tried to escape, but that thing just keeps bringing us back in here. It doesn't want to eat us, but it doesn't want us to leave. We have no idea why we are here!"

"Well we think Pherra has been taken care of." Jake crossed his fingers across his neck to symbolise she could be dead.

Herman and Gavin looked at one another, and the stranger smiled.

"So that is what all those explosions were about, Parts of the soil in here have been falling down onto us," Herman stated as another lot of soil hit him on the head.

"We need to leave now!" Cassie gestured to the way out.

Herman and the stranger stood up, and headed towards the front of the cave. When they reached the entrance they could not believe the devastation around them. The whole place was on fire; it was like a scene out of Dante's Inferno. Everything was burning fast. The scene was a red burning fire, but this time it was carnage. Suddenly they saw there was a small clearing in the trees on the far side of the opening; it could be made out when the wind changed direction just for a split second. Then it seemed to disappear into the flames.

"This way!" shouted Jake, who led the way towards the clearing. They ran as fast as they could. The sound of the fighter jet overhead could still be heard. *Is Pherra really down? If she is, wouldn't the fighter jet return to base?* he thought to himself.

Reaching the clearing, they headed farther into the woods. The heat from the fires was intense, causing them to sweat profusely. Everyone followed Jake's lead by covering up their faces with clothing to minimise how much smoke they were breathing in. Smoke inhalation was a deadly killer; they had come too far.

"We need to keep going this way, where the fires are not burning," shouted Jake.

The group followed in a single file line, until Jake froze in place. In front of him was Pherra, lying on the ground with her eyes closed. Her wings were spread out and there was the outline of scorched earth around her. *Is she breathing? Is she dead, or is it a ploy to lure them in?* Jake thought to himself.

"Do you think she is dead?" whispered Cassie in a tiny voice in case she was indeed not dead.

"I don't know, but we can't take any chances. Everyone follow me and be extra quiet."

Slowly and quietly, they started to sneak around the downed phoenix. As they did, they watched very carefully where they placed their feet; the last thing they needed to do was make a whole lot of noise. Pherra was enormously larger than anyone could have really imagined. This was the closest that Jake and Cassie had got to Pherra. It was a process that was seeming to take forever to get around her. Pherra did not look like she was breathing, lying very still and motionless. Jake had managed to get by first and he stopped to watch the others come through.

Gavin, who was in the middle of the group, lost his footing and slipped. He went crashing into Pherra's head with an almighty thud. Pherra suddenly awakened, her eyes opening and her head jolting with force. Jake could see that Gavin had frozen in place, he was staring at her open eye. Jake could see the beads of sweat developing on Gavin's forehead. He had to get his friend away *now*!

"It's awake! Get away!" screamed Gavin, not realising that Herman and the stranger had run past to get themselves to safety. Gavin was knocked flying to the floor as Pherra stood up. She leaned forward and glared at Gavin as he held his breath for dear life.

"Gavin, come on move" screamed out Jake. Gavin remained frozen in place, Pherra's breath causing his hair to blow back. Her huge wings opened and then she took to the heavens above. Gavin was frozen in place. Jake and Cassie ran over to their friend.

"Gavin, Gavin. Are you okay?" Jake started to shake Gavin's shoulders until he came to his senses.

"Why did she not take him?" Cassie verbalised what she was wondering to Jake.

"I don't know, but I'm guessing she will be back again." Shaking his head, Jake looked at where Pherra had been lying.

Pherra flew high and higher into the distance and was soon out of view. Powering through the sky, the fighter jet flew overhead, clearly in pursuit of Pherra.

THE GROUP HAD MANAGED TO GET TO THE outskirts of the woods. Cassie, Jake, Josie, Gavin, Herman, and the stranger were totally exhausted. The fires continued to rage around them—all they could see were the plumes of billowing smoke. It was burning everything to a crisp. There was no letting up; they needed to get to safety.

"What do we do now?" Jake questioned as he pointed to the fire around them.

Josie looked at the gauntlet. "It's not over until I find Andy."

"Well, I am getting the hell out of here." shouted Jake

"As am I," Herman and the stranger chorused as they ventured off in their own direction.

"Ah, man." Gavin struggled to keep up with Jake, Cassie, and Josie.

In the distance a fighter jet circled above as if it was surveying the ground below. Cassie, Jake, Josie, and Gavin jogged into the farmer's field. They were all filthy, covered in soot, mud, and anything else that they had experienced in the woods. The sound of fire engines could be heard behind them. Suddenly, they stopped and looked to see about twenty fire trucks pull up to the woods.

As they continued on their journey to find Pherra, the plane suddenly turned and started to head towards them.

"Guys, why is that thing flying this way?" wailed Gavin.

Pherra was flying towards the jet. The group ducked down onto the dirty earth below them as the jet launched another assault. Pherra dodged the heat seeking missile, but it turned to track its target. It caught up with Pherra, hitting her, causing a gigantic explosion. Pherra again came tumbling down to the ground, but this time she got straight back up and flew up higher and higher. She chased after the fighter jet. The hunter was now the hunted. She flew effortlessly through the sky, giving chase with no sign of injury. The jet could not appear to shake Pherra.

Suddenly, she then went into a lunge movement, just like an eagle, and caught the rear wing of the jet with her taloned claws. There was a burst of light as the pilot pressed his ejector seat. Pherra dragged the aircraft down to the ground, causing it to burst into flames.

She let out an almighty roar, triumphant and strong. Josie could see the ejected pilot in the sky. He had activated his parachute. Pherra noticed this and moved to grab the pilot. Josie raised her hand as fast as light, as she aimed and fired. The most intense amount of blue energy appeared that she had ever seen. Her power had doubled—she was at full strength. Josie aimed to hit Pherra. The huge bolt of energy flew through the sky, hitting her hard in the back, and she came crashing down to the ground, creating a large, smouldering crater.

"Josie, you did it. She is down!" exclaimed Jake in excitement.

Apparently Josie wasn't convinced as she headed over to the crater to check for herself. Pherra had taken full on impacts from some very heavy artillery and had just brushed them off.

When Josie reached the site, she could see that Pherra was hurt; she was still breathing, but much more slowly and shallow.

Josie raised her hand, ready to finish off Pherra, when suddenly, Cassie jumped in front of her.

"Wait, stop!"

"Get out of the way. I'm going to finish this once and for all before anyone else gets—"

"What if she doesn't want to hurt anyone? What if she just wants to go home?" asked Cassie.

Raising her head, Pherra looked directly as Josie before dropping her head back down. Josie lowered her arm. She could not kill a helpless animal, even one as dangerous as Pherra.

The very ground beneath them then began to shake, and a round, glowing circle appeared in the air. Within the circle there was the Dark Goblin who was holding *The Spellmaster's Book* firmly in his grip.

"It's you!" shouted Josie, who then fired a blast of blue energy towards the Dark Goblin, since he was the one who was responsible for her missing brother. The energy hit the portal, but bounced off.

"You cannot hurt me here even with your gauntlet," laughed the Dark Goblin.

Josie was getting redder and redder in the face, anger rising inside of her. She knew the Dark Goblin was the key to finding Andy. "Where is my brother, you ugly, disgusting piece of vermin?"

The Dark Goblin's grin widened. "He is safe, here with me in the world of Mytherios."

Pherra stood back up. She looked at the group, and then she noticed the Dark Goblin. Flapping her wings, she flew through the portal that the Dark Goblin had opened. Josie moved towards the portal, but as she got closer it was suddenly gone. The Dark Goblin had closed the portal and had gotten away again, this time taking Pherra with him.

Josie fell down to her knees, screaming at the top of her lungs.

Jake raced over to her and placed his hand on her shoulders. "You will get him back, there will be another way, I am sure."

Josie rose onto her feet. She was shivering and sniffling. Wiping away her tears, she turned to the others. "Thank you, for all of your help." She then gave everyone in the group a hug. "I have to go now, I need to find Andy." Josie ran off into the distance, before slowly vanishing out of sight.

"Can we go home now?" moaned Gavin.

"Sure, let's go home," replied Jake. They all made their way back to Jake's car, where Gavin and Cassie had to share a seat together. Jake started his engine and headed back into town. The roads were now quiet, but the destruction was horrific. Buildings had all their windows broken, the church tower was heavily damaged—its spire had been broken—and buildings were charred from the fire.

"How long do you think it will take for all of this to be cleaned up?" asked Cassie.

"I don't know, but together we will help our town rebuild. Pherra is gone. This is our chance to build up and strengthen up if she was ever to return."

In the land of Mytherios, Andy was lost. He left the beach and made his way around the large forest where he met the red-haired fairy.

"Hello, is anyone there?" He hadn't seen anyone in the few hours that he had been lost in Mytherios, he was beginning to worry that he was alone. But back in the real world this was a few months. Andy was getting tired and needed somewhere to rest. Seeing an entrance to a cave, he decided to take shelter there. He made his way inside ... only to stop and stare at all the human remains that were dumped in the entrance. His heart was pounding in his chest as he ran back out. Standing in front of him was the fairy he had met in the forest.

"I have already told you, you do not belong here." She pointed to the ground.

"But where am I supposed to go?" As Andy stepped towards the fairy, he found himself back on the beach where he started.

Andy looked at the water, and could hear the growl of what sounded like a Kraken. He looked closer to see large tentacles pierce the surface. He had seen pictures of these in a book at home, now he was convinced that there was a Kraken lurking in the depths.

Sitting down on the sandy beach, he placed his head in his hands. He had no idea what he could do or where he could go!

"How will I ever get home?" he asked himself.

A crackle and burst of bright light caught Andy's attention.

High in the sky, he could see a portal opening. Out flew the enormous bird he had seen the previous day. He watched as it flew through the sky, heading back to the volcano from which it came forth. The bird paid no attention to Andy sitting on the beach, it just continued to soar to its volcano until it was nothing more than a tiny spec in the sky.

"I really need to get out of here."

There was a sudden cackle from a familiar voice.

The Dark Goblin had been listening in. Andy ignored the laugh and stared out to sea, hoping that one day he would finally find his way home.

SIX MONTHS LATER, back in the small town which experienced Pherra's fury, life was returning to normal. Jake's Camaro was fixed and his relationship with Cassie was blossoming. The church tower had been repaired, and all the windows in the buildings replaced.

The woodland fire was extinguished, but the damage was still apparent. It was going to be there for some time. Gavin moved out of town, his parents worried that the phoenix may one day return and wreak havoc upon the town once more.

Cassie and Jake rarely spoke about Pherra, as they did not want to endure any more nightmares about what happened during those few days. But there was one thing that they struggled to forget and that was Josie.

One evening, when Cassie and Jake were having a get together at Jake's, the conversation turned to Josie.

"Where do you think she could be now?" Cassie asked Jake.

"You mean Josie? I don't know. But I do hope that wherever she is she finally found her brother."

"Do you ever think about that day, the fires?" asked Cassie.

Jake dropped his head down and looked at the floor. "I try not to, but I still get nightmares. It's so hard not to think about it ... the pilots who lost their lives and how I almost lost you that day."

"I understand. I'm sorry that I put you in that position. But I just couldn't give up on Gavin. I know you can understand that."

Jake smiled at Cassie and gave her a hug. His phone then went off and he picked it up to see a message from Gavin. The message contained a link to a website. He clicked the link and gasped when he saw what it said.

"Jake, what's wrong?" Cassie could see the fear taking over Jake's entire body as he turned deadly pale.

He handed her the phone, and Cassie read the story. She dropped the phone onto the floor in shock. The story read:

The demon is here, he brings hell's fire and brimstone with him. So far he has taken over the town and there is nothing we can do to stop him. He has claws like nothing anyone has ever seen

before. The town is overrun. Please stay away, there is a serious threat and danger to life.

Cassie stared at Jake. He tried to speak but the words wouldn't come. Finally regaining his composure, he began to talk. "A demon? That town is only an hour away from here."

"What are we going to do?"

"Ignore it! We're going to do nothing. I'm not going to try and take on a demon, who is bringing nothing but hell's fury with it."

"Jake, we cannot sit by. We have to help them."

Jake could see that there was no way Cassie was going to let him do nothing. Picking up his phone off the floor, he copied the message, then sent it to Cassie's phone. "Pass me your phone, Cassie."

"Why?" she asked, confused.

"Trust me."

Cassie gave Jake a very intrigued stare as Jake clicked on the message he sent to her phone. He opened up her contacts; Josie's number was still in her list of contacts. The message was ready, pausing briefly he hit send.

Almost immediately Cassie's phone rang. It was Josie. Jake answered the call and put it on loudspeaker.

"Thank you for your message, I will look into this

right away. This time I will go alone, please do not try to help." The phone then went dead, Josie had gone.

Jake placed his arms around Cassie as they looked out the window to see everyone going about their daily lives. The Demon was coming, but Josie was out there to put an end to the mysterious being that wanted nothing but destruction.

THE END

If you enjoyed *Pherra Rises*, please check out *Claws of the Demon*, Book Three in the Legends of Mytherios.

See more at www.JamesKeith.co.uk

ABOUT THE AUTHOR

James Keith is a knowledgeable professional with almost 20 years of proficiency in the healthcare industry. James has always been an activist for mental health due to his own experiences in the field.

James wants people to be aware of how to deal with emotional, psychological, and social well-being issues and how to stop them from affecting their lives.

**Follow James at
www.JamesKeith.co.uk**

facebook.com/jameskeith86
twitter.com/JamesKeith86
instagram.com/jamesikeith